I0626268

HOT SUMMER NIGHTS

ROSE MARIE MEUWISSEN

Hot Summer Nights

by
Rose Marie Meuwissen

Hot Summer Nights
Digital/Print Edition
Copyright 2013 by Rose Marie Meuwissen
https://www.rosemariemeuwissen.com

Hot Summer Nights is a work of fiction. Names, characters, and incidents depicted in this book are products of the author's imagination or are used fictitiously. Any resemblance to actual events, locales, organizations, or persons, living or dead, is entirely coincidental and beyond the intent of the author or the publisher. No part of this book may be reproduced or transmitted in any form or by any means, electronic or mechanical, including photocopying, recording, or by any information storage and retrieval system, without permission in writing from the publisher.

NO GHOSTWRITERS WERE USED IN THE CREATION OF THIS BOOK. THIS WORK OF FICTION IS 100% THE ORIGINAL WORK OF ROSE MARIE MEUWISSEN.

ISBN: 978-0-9903788-5-3
Published in the United States of America
Nordic Publishing
Edited by Nancy Schumacher
Cover Design by Rose Marie Meuwissen

✺ Created with Vellum

To all the matches made through internet dating services that have led to lasting relationships which have offered many divorcees a second chance at love.

PRIOR LAKE

HOT SUMMER NIGHTS

When the boat Rycca Peterson was awarded in her divorce settlement, an internet dating site her best friends signed her up on and her twenty year class reunion are determined she meet Dan Johnston, who is she to say no?

A MINNESOTA LAKES ROMANCE

PRIOR LAKE

MINNESOTA

Land of 10,000 Lakes

HOT SUMMER NIGHTS

By

Rose Marie Meuwissen

CHAPTER 1

Rycca Petersen stood on the dock looking out over the lake, fixated on the many boats skimming across the water. Then she turned to look at her own boat sitting idly in the boat lift. Yes, it was her boat now. The problem was she was scared to death to take it out on the lake. She was a grown woman; she'd driven a car for years! How hard could it be to drive a boat? Really hard when you had no clue how to do it. Which was why she took the boating class offered by the City of Prior Lake a few weeks earlier and to her surprise passed it with flying colors. Now, actually doing it was another whole thing.

She took a deep breath, and grabbed a hold of the large wheel to crank the boat down into the water. That was more than likely the easiest part of taking out the boat. She put her beach bag and cooler in the boat before getting in. Next, she put the key in and started the engine. Rycca sighed as she heard the engine running. A part of her wished it wouldn't start because then she could just go back and sit on the beach in her chair. But no such luck, it was running and she was going to have to follow through with this. She made sure the dock ropes were all untied, put the boat in reverse and backed out of the slip. So far so good! At least she hadn't hit anything yet, which was her greatest fear.

It was the Fourth of July and a lot of boats were on the water. Rycca drove slowly through the channel, increasing the speed once she was in the open water and proceeded to the other side of the island directly ahead of her in the lake where she could drop the anchor and hopefully relax. Until, of course, it was time to go back home and she would have to get it back into the boat lift. She would worry about that later.

Rycca found a spot she liked, put the boat in neutral, let the anchor down quickly until it hit bottom and then tied the boat off. She turned the engine off after making sure her cell phone was in her bag. Just in case she needed to call someone for help. But, unfortunately, she had no idea who she would call. She turned on the radio to her favorite station and sat down.

She was a nervous wreck because of the stupid boat. Rycca wanted the boat, mainly because she didn't want *him* to have the boat. And now it had been a year since her divorce and today was the first time she had taken it out. Oh well, she was out on the lake now and she had done it!

She pulled out her towel and laid it out on the back of the boat, pulled on her visor and laid down on the towel to read her romance novel. She loved reading romance novels because they always had happy endings, and she so wanted to believe in someone getting the happy ending, even if it wasn't her.

Rycca'd had enough of men and their lies for the time being, which was why she hadn't dated anyone since her divorce. Maybe next year. Maybe later. Unfortunately, for all the other men out there, she just wasn't sure she could trust men ever again. The only one she did trust was her son, who was working in Texas doing an internship for the summer, or she may have been able to have him take her out on the boat.

Once Rycca was comfortable, she looked around at the other boats nearby. Just as she looked directly across at the boat next to her, she saw a man alone on a sleek red speedboat staring her way. He sported a nice dark tan on his definitely toned chest. She couldn't tell if he was looking at her since he wore dark sunglasses. She only hoped he couldn't tell she was assessing him through her dark glasses. He had black hair, cut short. Why was she even assessing him? She had no idea. She wasn't interested in meeting anyone at this time. He walked over to the back of his boat, stepped down on the platform and dove into the water.

Rycca resumed her reading, while ignoring the man swimming in the water between their boats. A few minutes after he dove in, she felt drops of water sprinkle her warm skin and immediately looked up wondering if it had started to rain.

"Sorry. Did I get you wet?"

Her glance darted to the water where the man from the boat beside her treaded water, looking at her apologetically.

"That's okay. It felt good," Rycca said, wishing she could just jump in to cool off. She could, of course, but now that he was in the water, it would seem a bit too forward for her comfort.

"The water is nice. It's really a hot one today."

Was he asking her to join him? Hell if she knew. Now what was she supposed to do? She was hot so she got up and moved over to sit on the step on the back of her boat so she could put her legs in the water to cool off. Rycca could feel his eyes watching her. She didn't turn his way. Minutes later, he was in front of her looking right up at her.

"My name is Dan Johnston. I hail from one of these

houses on Prior Lake," he said, pointing across the lake, where several houses dotted the shoreline.

He obviously was intent on talking to her. "Nice to meet you. My name is Rycca. I also hail from one of the many houses on Prior Lake," she said.

"So did I convince you to jump in?" he asked.

Without answering, Rycca rose to her feet and dove in. Minutes later, coming to the water's surface, she swam over to her boat and held on to the boat's steps.

Dan swam over towards Rycca. "Welcome to the cool lake water," he said.

"It is nice. Very refreshing." Rycca was feeling a bit uneasy since he was being so in her face. She used her boat steps to get out of the water and sat down on the back platform.

"Is this a new way to meet women these days?" Rycca asked.

"Not sure. This is the first time I tried it. How is it working?" Dan asked and grinned at Rycca.

"Haven't decided yet. Depends what your goal is?" Rycca answered.

"I'd love to get your phone number and call you. Maybe we could have dinner sometime."

"I think that may be a bit difficult," she stated.

"Why?" he asked.

"I could give you my business card, but the water may present a small problem," Rycca replied, even though she wasn't sure if she would give it to him or not.

"Valid point."

"You never asked if I was married," Rycca stated.

"Are you?" Dan asked. "I didn't see a ring."

"No. Divorced," she answered. "How about you?"

"No. Widower."

What the hell, he was definitely easy on the eyes. Maybe it was time to try dating. He seemed harmless. Being a realtor for years, her phone number was plastered all over town anyway so what could it hurt to give him her business card or number?

"Sorry about your wife." Rycca stared into his eyes to be sure he was sincere and not just telling her some story. She had learned a lot about people over the years and was able to read them pretty well, which was why her ex-husband, Steve, hadn't had a chance when he tried lying to her about his affair with her real estate closer, Angie McDonald. "When you're ready to leave, pull over to the side of my boat and I'll give you my business card." With that, Rycca got back up on her boat and lay back down on her towel to dry off in the sun.

Dan realized he'd been dismissed. "Okay. I'll be stopping by when I get ready to leave." He swam back over to his boat and lay down on the back of it to dry off. He had no idea what he was doing. Or what had gotten into him. He'd never been this forward with a perfect stranger before. But when he saw her remove her cover-up, and stand before him in her tiny bikini, he had thought of nothing but meeting her. No matter what the method. And there was something about her name, Rycca, that seemed so familiar to him.

Rycca tried to concentrate on the romance book she was reading, but it was really difficult when she knew there was a very hot guy on the next boat who was interested in her, and probably staring at her at that very minute. Finally, she set the book down, closed her eyes, and listened to the song playing on the radio. The song just happened to be, *I Will*

Survive. How appropriate! She became lost in the song and the ones that followed and slowly drifted off to sleep.

Sometime later, Rycca woke up abruptly and sat up. The voice on the radio announced it was five o'clock. She really should get going. Dan's boat was still anchored beside her. Good. She glanced his way and found him watching her. She was okay with that and started putting her towel away, stowing her bag and cooler under the dash on the passenger side. She put her cover-up back on. He had enough time to see the goods which she was very proud of, especially since she put her time in a couple of times a week at the Dakota Fitness Club. This would be the tricky part, where she needed to start the boat and get the anchor up.

Rycca couldn't help holding her breath as she stood and turned the key to start the boat. Nothing was what she heard. The boat didn't start. Now what was she going to do?

"Need some help?" Dan called over to her.

"It's not starting." Rycca sat down in the driver's seat.

"It might be you drained the battery by playing the radio. I can jump start it if you have jumper cables or I can just tow you back to your dock."

Rycca walked over to the side of her boat so she could see him. "No cables."

Dan pulled his boat up alongside her and handed her a rope.

"Not to sound dumb but how will this work? How do I steer the boat if it's not running?"

"All you have to do is hold on to the rope and your boat will follow. When we get to your dock, you'll just have to grab hold of the dock. I'll tie mine up and come and help you once we get there."

Rycca walked to the front of her boat with the rope and tied it to the cleat. Dan pulled forward to tighten up the slack and began pulling her boat behind his. This would only happen to her. How were you supposed to enjoy sitting in the boat if you couldn't even play the radio? They were almost to the Cove, which was the marina and beach area for her housing association.

"It's right ahead. My slip is on the end, on the left side of the dock," Rycca yelled to Dan.

She watched him maneuver his boat in that direction and turn sharply away.

"Untie the rope, now," Dan called.

Rycca untied the rope and grabbed a hold of the dock. At least she'd made it back. She realized she was so relieved to be back at her own dock that she hadn't even moved when she saw Dan walk up the dock, take hold of the front of her boat and pull it into the lift. It was enough to break her trance, and she helped pull the boat in place. Rycca put the cooler and bag on the dock, grabbed the key out of the ignition, and stepped up to get out of the boat as Dan's hand reached out to help her. She stood on the dock face to face with this very hot man whose darkly tanned chest and six pack abs were way too close to her barely covered bikini clad body. Wow! Thank heavens she had put her cover up back on. What was going on with her? She hadn't felt this attracted to any guy in a long time. She released his hand.

"Thanks for helping me. I really appreciate it," Rycca said making eye contact with Dan.

He beamed. "No problem. Glad I was there to help you." He walked over and turned the wheel to raise the boat up in the lift.

Rycca reached into her bag and pulled a business card out of her wallet. She held out her hand to him as he turned back toward her. "I told you I would give you this earlier."

Dan smiled. "I thought maybe you forgot about our earlier conversation."

"No. Kind of freaked out when the boat wouldn't start though."

"That's fine. Happens to the best of us. I'll call you," he said. "Well, I best get going. Talk to you later." He walked back over to his boat and jumped in.

Rycca walked behind him. "Thanks again," she said.

Dan looked up at her from the driver's seat of his boat. "I know it's the 4th and you probably have plans but if you don't, would you like to have dinner at Captain Jack's restaurant on Prior Lake? It'll be a nice night to have dinner on the lake."

"Well, I was maybe going to meet up with some friends later, but I don't think I feel like driving over to Lake Minnetonka to meet them. Sure. I owe you for helping me," Rycca said.

"Sounds good. I could pick you up or you can meet me there," Dan said.

"I'll meet you there."

"Seven?"

"That will work. See you then," Rycca said.

Dan started his boat and pulled away from the dock. He waved as he sped off.

Rycca waved back, then headed to the beach and up to her house. What was she doing? She had a date with some guy she didn't even know. Oh well, she needed to eat dinner and she really hadn't wanted to drive to Lake Minnetonka anyway. She took a shower and dressed in a pair of shorts and a low cut top. She spent extra time with her makeup. Might as well make a good impression, as long as she was going out on a date. She slipped on heeled sandals and drove up to Captain Jack's restaurant on Prior Lake.

CHAPTER 2

Dan was pumped as he drove the boat back to his dock. Rycca was one hot chick and even looked better up close. He hadn't had any plans for tonight, and he was excited to get to know her over dinner. If he was lucky maybe he could talk her into watching the fireworks they shot off on Prior Lake. He was a huge fan of fireworks, especially good ones, and Prior Lake was known for having an awesome display. Only one thing bothered him about Rycca, there was something very familiar about her name, but he couldn't put his finger on it. He hadn't really dated for a while, just a few dinners here and there after his wife died. It was just plain hard to meet women who appealed to him, especially in his line of work. Being the president of an old local bank made it difficult to do the dating circles. Recently, his buddies suggested he try one of the online dating services, so he finally signed up late the night before but hadn't even had time to look at potential matches. Maybe he wouldn't need to after tonight.

After showering, he dressed in jeans and a t-shirt, and splashed on his best sexy cologne. He walked into the garage not sure which car to take. He didn't want to show off too much on the first date, or did he? He chose the pick-up truck, to be on the safe side, instead of the Corvette or the 69 Chevy Camaro and headed up to Captain Jack's restaurant on Prior Lake to meet his date. The first one in quite a while.

There was a lot to be said for driving herself on a date, especially with someone she didn't really know; if it didn't go well she could leave. Hopefully it would at least be tolerable. He seemed like a nice guy. After all, he did help her get the stupid boat back into the boat slip and the lift back up. After today she wasn't so sure she was ever going to take the boat out again. She should probably just sell the thing and be done with it. Rycca pulled into the parking lot of Captain Jack's restaurant on Prior Lake and got the last available parking spot. She hated this part. She had no idea if his car was already in the parking lot or not, if he was there or not. So she could either wait a while and go in fashionably late, or take her chances by going in alone and waiting conspicuously, if he wasn't. Her nerves got the best of her. She parked and went in.

Dan was waiting patiently by the door when Rycca walked in. He unconsciously gave her the once over and walked toward her. "Right on time. The hostess will be right back to seat us."

Rycca couldn't help smiling. He seemed so genuine. Oh, he'd assessed her when she walked in, but heck, he was a guy and that's what guys did. She felt confident she looked good and passed the test. The hostess came back and they followed her to a table with a view of the lake. The waitress handed them each menus and left.

"I haven't been up here this summer yet," Rycca stated.

"I stop up regularly. Their burgers are good." Dan smiled and made eye contact with Rycca.

"I think I'll have a burger then." Rycca wasn't up for making small talk with a stranger, but she was going to give it her best shot. Mainly because she felt she owed him for helping her get her boat back to the dock. But she was tired of being alone and probably some male companionship was just what she needed.

"I'm really glad I took my boat out this afternoon so I could be sitting across from you right now." Dan grinned her way.

"No offense or anything, but I hope I don't have to go through that experience again."

"Save a damsel in distress and this is the thanks I get," Dan joked.

"Sorry, I guess that didn't come out right. It's just that I have issues with the boat," Rycca stated.

"I see."

"Mostly that I'm scared to death of the stupid thing. You, of course, had no way of knowing that was the first time I'd ever taken it out."

"That explains everything."

"Pretty much."

They ordered burgers and beers and watched the boats pull up to dock. People were in a celebrating mood since it was the 4th of July.

"Your business card said you are a realtor. So how's the real estate business these days? Are houses selling again?" Dan asked.

"I've been doing it a long time, so I'm doing okay. The market is picking up too which helps."

"That's good to hear. The economy needs the housing market to start moving again."

"So what do you do?" Rycca asked.

"I'm in banking," he answered.

"Oh, which bank?"

"Prior Lake State Bank."

"That's nice. You don't have a long drive to go to work."

"I think I'm a bit spoiled on that count." Dan beamed.

"What department do you work in?"

"Management."

So he had a decent job at least. Even though he didn't say what department he was a manager of, he must make good money. Not that a large salary was a prerequisite for a boyfriend, but it sure helped.

Their food came. They ate and finished their beers. It was only about eight o'clock and she was dreading the thought of walking down to the lake to watch the fireworks alone. Would she be considered too forward if she asked him to join her? Heck, she had no idea what the dating rules were these days; it had been over 20 years since she'd gone on a date.

"Are you planning on watching the fireworks on the lake tonight?" Dan asked.

"We have a great view from my beach. They shoot them off right across the lake from there. Best seats on the lake. I love seeing all the boats anchored in the water with their lights on. With a clear sky, it is breathtaking to see the stars in the sky and the red, green, and white lights on the boats in the water."

"Should be a great night for fireworks. It looks like the weather is going to cooperate. Clear skies are in the forecast."

"Do you have a good view from your house?" Rycca asked.

"Not really. Would you like some company?"

Rycca didn't know what to say. She certainly would love to not have to go down to the lake tonight by herself, but it just plain felt weird. But what the heck? She was probably in more danger going alone. "Sure. You're not busy? No plans for the evening?"

"I am supposed to be up in Nisswa, but things got hectic and I decided I really didn't want to spend six hours on the road driving up there. Especially when I'd rather spend those six hours relaxing on my own boat on Prior Lake," Dan stated and took a drink of beer.

"Makes perfect sense to me. That's why I built my house on Prior Lake. I always hated driving up to Brainerd, where my parents have a cabin. And the traffic coming back is always horrible."

"Exactly," Dan agreed.

"You probably realized my house is part of an Association when you were down at the dock. There will probably be many families down there. Unfortunately, there will be a lot of mosquitoes down there too."

"Should I bring anything?"

"Just a chair."

Dan paid the check and they walked out to the parking lot. He walked her to her car. She got in her Sebring convertible, on which she'd left the top down.

"I'll meet you at the lake in should we say about half an hour? I usually sit on the hill by one of the deck platforms, so just look for me there. I'm going to put some long pants on and grab a jacket so the mosquitoes don't get the best of me."

"Good idea. See you down there." Dan walked to his truck and Rycca backed out and drove home.

Rycca checked her phone when she got home and saw that Shelly, one of her friends she was supposed to meet tonight, had called. She returned the call.

"Shelly, where are you guys at?" Rycca asked.

"We're at Lord Fletchers, which is where you should be. There are hot guys here everywhere."

"You know I'm not really into that scene yet."

"Exactly the reason Tara and I signed you up on the Metro Singles Dating website last night."

"Seriously? I have no interest in meeting men on the internet."

"Hey, at least take a look and see if anyone interests you, okay? It won't kill you to look."

"Whatever."

"I emailed you all the info so take a look tonight while you are sitting home all alone."

The background noise increased as it sounded like the band started playing. "Shelly? I can't hear you anymore."

"Got to go, I'll call you tomorrow."

The call disconnected before Rycca could tell Shelly about her dinner date and, she wasn't sure what to call it, a fireworks date? Oh well, she set the phone down, ran upstairs, and put on a pair of jeans. She grabbed a light windbreaker jacket, a cooler with a couple of wine coolers and went through the garage to get a folding chair in a bag. She hung the bag on her shoulder, closed the garage door and walked down to the lake.

Thankfully, most people preferred to sit down by the beach so the deck was open, but she decided to set her chair on the path next to it so she could watch for Dan. Minutes later, she saw a man walking up the hill. The sun had just set so it was hard to see if it was him until he was almost all the way up the hill.

"Just in time," she said.

"This is a great spot," Dan said as he took his chair out of the bag and set it up next to her chair.

"I told you," she said. Rycca reached into her cooler, pulled out two wine coolers and handed one to him. "Sorry, this was the only thing in my frig."

Dan took the bottle from her. "Thanks, this will work."

In the next five minutes, the beach filled with families to

watch the fireworks. People were setting off their own fire-works on the beach too, so there was an array of whizzing, popping and exploding going on as a pre-show. Then the fireworks started across the lake. The sky lit up in beautiful sparkling colors as they were shot into the air while the lake was an array of green and red lights from all the boats anchored in the water to watch the show.

"I love watching the fireworks right here. This has to be one of the best displays around. And for me it is ideal."

"Why is that?"

"I didn't have to drive anywhere and have to fight to get a parking spot, all I had to do was walk about half a block."

"Sounds like the ideal way to watch fireworks."

The finale began with a rapid succession of fireworks shot in the air along with a couple of big boomers.

Rycca felt awkward as soon as the finale ended. She didn't know if she was expected to invite him up to her house, but it didn't really matter because she didn't feel comfortable doing that so she didn't. And tomorrow was a work day, which she could use as an excuse. So they sat and talked while the rest of the people walked by them on their way back to their houses. Fifteen minutes later, they were the only ones left sitting on the hill and the beach was empty.

"Looks like we have the lake to ourselves. Want to walk down to the beach?" Dan asked as he searched her face for an answer.

"Sure. Beautiful hot summer nights with clear skies and moonlight don't come along real often."

Dan extended his hand to her as they walked down the steps to the lake. Rycca hesitated at first, but placed her hand in his. After all, it was dark and she didn't want to fall. They got to the beach, walked over to the dock and sat down on the edge.

"How long have you been divorced?" Dan asked.

"Little over a year."

"Have you started dating again?"

"No, this is the first time," Rycca answered. "When did your wife die?"

"About two years ago. She lost her battle with breast cancer."

"So when did you start dating again?"

"About a year ago, I decided I should probably get out and meet some women."

"How has that been working out?"

"I went on a few dinner dates, that's about all. It's hard to meet the right people."

"I suppose. I don't even know where to begin to meet eligible men. And then both people have to be interested and have some common interests."

"Exactly. Not like you can ask for a life resume."

Rycca laughed. "No, but that might not be a bad idea."

"Why did you get divorced?"

"My husband cheated with a work acquaintance of mine. Guess I'm kind of gun-shy of that happening again."

"Not all guys cheat. I never once cheated on my wife and we were married for twenty years."

"That's good to know," Rycca said.

"Rycca, you are a beautiful woman. And I'm extremely attracted to you. Men will find you attractive. I'd be interested in going out with you." Dan reached over to gently caress her cheek.

"You're definitely a good looking guy. I'm sure all the women want to go out with you."

"Not all. Besides, there has to be chemistry and that doesn't always happen." Dan gently kissed Rycca's lips.

Rycca opened to the kiss. Hell it had been over a year since she'd been kissed. In fact, the last time was her husband. This was different. Totally different and she liked it. Her whole body reacted to the kiss. Hell, she actually wanted to have sex with this man. Just from one kiss. This probably wasn't good. She wouldn't of course, at least not tonight anyway. But she could certainly enjoy some kissing. She kissed him back. The more he kissed her she became less sure that having sex tonight shouldn't be an option. The kiss ended and Dan was caressing her face with his eyes.

She stood up to break the mood. "It's getting late and tomorrow is a work day."

Dan stood up, took her hand and they walked silently back up the hill to their chairs. They put the chairs back in their bags.

"Rycca, I had a great time today. Can I call you?"

She looked up into his eyes—eyes that looked kind yet full of passion. The kiss topped the charts in her book. There was no way she would say no to going out with him again. "Yes, I'd like that." She saw the relief in his face when she answered.

"Would you like me to walk you to your house?"

As much as Rycca would've liked to say yes, she knew she couldn't because it would be way too hard to not ask him in. "I'll be fine. Thanks anyway."

"Okay. Thanks for a great evening. I'll give you a call." He picked up his chair, walked back down the steps and over to where he had parked his truck on the street.

Rycca walked the rest of the way up the hill to the street and down to her house. It had been a long day. She was tired and she had a busy day tomorrow so she got ready for bed as soon as she entered the house. She was too tired to check out the dating sight Shelly had put her on, and maybe she wouldn't even need it now anyway, so she went to sleep.

Dan was ecstatic when he arrived home. Today was the best day he'd had in a very long time. Rycca seemed so genuine, a real person, not one of those fake women who wanted to date him for his social status and money. Heck, she didn't even know who he really was or how much he made. Rycca liked him for him, and that was what he wanted. They still had a lot of getting to know each other to do, but he was confident that part would go well.

He turned on his laptop to check his emails and found an email from the Metro Singles Dating site for which he'd just signed up. It said they had matches for him to look at. He had figured this would be a good way to meet women without them knowing who he was up front. Hopefully, he wouldn't need it now that he'd met Rycca. He clicked on the link to the website. Might as well take a look at his matches. He was, after all, curious as to how well this worked, and if he would even find any of them interesting. He signed into the site and clicked on matches. His number one match came up. He read the screen name—Prior Lake Woman, and stared at a picture of Rycca. What were the odds? He scrolled down and read her profile. Next, her interests. Wow! They were even a better match than he first thought. He couldn't stop thinking about her. He didn't even bother to look at the rest of his matches. Sometimes you just know, and he had felt something when he first saw her pull her boat up beside his. He would call her tomorrow and set up a date for the weekend. He had plans for Saturday night though so it would have to be Friday or Sunday.

CHAPTER 3

Rycca went into the office about ten. She had a closing at eleven with the Minnesota Titles office in Burnsville. She was forced to change title offices after the whole humiliating situation of her husband's affair with one of the agents at the old office.

She had a little time to kill before the closing so she turned on her laptop. Luckily, she had received an email from the dating site because she couldn't remember the name. She followed the link, but then had to go back to find the email from Shelly with her password. She signed in. Up came her profile and interests all filled out by Shelly and Tara. It didn't look too bad, they obviously knew her pretty well as it was uncanny how accurate it was. She scrolled down to matches. She wasn't sure why she was even doing this. She hated the whole idea of dating. Curiosity was getting the best of her though. It couldn't hurt to take a peek at who they thought were good matches for her.

Her number one match appeared on her screen. Unbelievable! What were the odds? It was Dan. His code name was 69 Camaro. Wow. He looked so hot in the picture she was beginning to think she was crazy to not have invited him up to the house. She scrolled down to the bio and interests. This was kind of like the life resume he had mentioned to her. They actually had many interests in common.

Now all she had to do was wait for him to call. Rycca looked at his picture again and wondered how many matches he'd received. Maybe he would be too busy taking out all the other matches to have time to go out with her. But then again maybe he wasn't really who she thought he was. Why hadn't he mentioned he was on a dating site? She powered down the computer. She had to get going to her appointment. She would just have to see if he called. Friday she had an out of town buyer she would be showing houses to, and Saturday was her twenty year class reunion at the Wild's Golf Club, so Sunday was the only day she had open.

After Rycca got home around five, her cell rang.

"Rycca how was your day?" Dan asked.

"Very good. Had a closing so it was payday."

"I've been thinking about you all day. Wanted to call to see if you are available on Friday night?"

"Sorry, I am showing houses to an out of town buyer on Friday night."

"Okay, how about Sunday?" he asked.

"Sunday works. What did you have in mind?" Rycca asked.

"I was thinking we could have brunch at Lord Fletchers to start and go from there."

"That sounds good."

"I'll pick you up at eleven."

"I'll be ready. Suppose you need the address though."

"I do need it to pick you up," he laughed.

"16000 Eagle Creek."

"I'm looking forward to seeing you again. I'll let you go for now."

"Okay, Sunday it is," Rycca said and hung up.

She was excited. He'd called and she had an actual date. She couldn't wait. All day she'd debated if she should tell Shelly about how she'd met Dan on the lake, and that he'd also showed up as a match on the dating site. She decided to wait till after their date on Sunday. Then she would be able to tell if it would go any further. Wouldn't she? Maybe? Ah, heck, she didn't have a clue how this dating thing worked. She would just wait and see how Sunday went.

CHAPTER 4

On Friday night after her client appointment, Rycca paced in front of her closet trying to decide what to wear to her class reunion. Of course, there wasn't anything in her closet that fit the bill. It was the dead of summer and hotter than heck. She needed a strappy, sexy, short little black dress. Only problem was she didn't have one. There was no choice but to go to the mall. Not how she planned to spend her Saturday morning, but there just wasn't any other solution. Unless of course she didn't go to the reunion, which had crossed her mind numerous times. She hadn't been close to many people in high school; her life-long friends were from college. But it was those friends who insisted she go. It just felt awkward to go now that she was divorced. But, she had already paid for it and, after all, it was just down the street at the Wilds Golf Club.

Late Saturday afternoon, Rycca went to her bedroom to get ready for the big night. Big night all right! She was now twenty years older than when she graduated from Burnsville High School. The only part that made her feel better was that everyone she graduated with was also twenty years older.

She put on her makeup, used the curling iron on her long blond hair to give it some body, and put on the perfect little black dress along with a matching new pair of sexy heeled sandals she'd picked up at the mall earlier. Her skin had picked up a nice tan from being out on the boat the other day. She added a necklace, earrings, bracelets and rings. Her finger still felt naked where her beautiful wedding ring used to sit. Thanks to her friends though, a beautifully designed ring set with the stones from her wedding ring sat on her right hand. Rycca took one last look at her reflection in the mirror and walked out to the garage. She got in her convertible and put the top up so her hair wouldn't be a mess by the time she arrived there.

A few minutes later, Rycca walked into the Wild's. She was greeted by a large sign that said, "Burnsville High School 20 year Class Reunion". Well at least she knew she was in the right place, so she walked up to the registration table to check in and get a name tag. She didn't recognize the person who asked her name, but saw her name tag said Sherry Thompson. Sadly, she didn't know many people as their class was large, about 800 students.

"Rycca Setterstrom," she stated. "Or Rycca Peterson. Not sure which one it's under."

"Maiden name. Rycca Setterstrom. Here you go," Sherry said handing her a name tag she could hang around her neck.

Rycca looked at her high school picture next to her name on the name tag. Wow, she looked so young. She put it on and walked over to look at the picture poster boards where there were little sheets to fill out your current info such as marital status, children, job, accomplishments etc. After she filled out her form, she pinned it on the board next to her picture and stopped to look at a few already up before heading into the ballroom. People were lined up at the bar to get drinks, and buffet tables were set up and waiting for the hot and cold entrees to be added. On the other end of the room, a band was getting ready to play. She remembered reading in the reunion invitation letter that the band members in the band, Lakers, were from their class.

This was beginning to seem like a very bad idea, as she didn't think she knew anyone who was there so far. Rycca walked over to the bar and got in line. A glass of wine in her hand would make her feel better. Minutes later, it was her turn and she ordered a glass of White Zinfandel. She handed the bartender the money, picked up her glass, turned to walk away and walked into a very manly chest. He smelled very good and her heart was racing as she looked up to see who she had just walked into. She froze in place and her mouth dropped open but nothing came out.

"Rycca."

"Dan," Rycca said as she backed up a step. "What are you doing here?"

"I guess we never talked about where we went to high school." Dan studied her face and eyes.

"I feel bad. Like I should have recognized you," Rycca said.

"Don't. We had a large class. I by no means knew everyone."

"I hate to admit it but I knew very few people. My ex went to a different high school and we dated all through high school so I think I spent more time at his high school events than Burnsville's." Rycca nervously readjusted her purse strap on her shoulder.

"I didn't recognize you but your name seemed familiar to me. I kept wondering why. Now I know why. We were in the same English class our senior year." He ordered a drink and they walked over to a table to sit down.

Rycca studied Dan as he sat beside her. He was such a handsome man. A part of her wondered why he hadn't asked her out for Saturday night, but since she was already going to the reunion, it hadn't mattered. Now she knew why. How odd this whole week had been. First the boat, then the dating site and now the reunion. Something was definitely pushing them together. It must be meant to be was the only thing Rycca could think of.

"Looks like we are destined to meet one way or the other," Dan said and picked up her hand. He admired the ring on her finger. "Very stunning ring. Must say I'm glad it's on your right hand."

"Thanks. I designed it and used the stones from my old wedding ring."

The band began playing. Dan and Rycca danced and when the slow song played, he took her in his arms and held her close as they moved to the music. After the song ended, they walked outside on the patio to cool off. Even though it was a hot summer night there was a nice breeze. They walked to the railing and Dan put his arms around her waist and pulled her towards him. He kissed her and she kissed him back. It felt so natural.

"I have to say I never thought there was anything to falling in love at first sight, but I do now. I think I knew you were the one for me when I first saw you pull up next to my boat. You feel so perfect in my arms," Dan whispered in her ear.

"I haven't been attracted to anyone besides my ex all these years, but I am definitely attracted to you. I actually thought about inviting you up to the house the other night but I was afraid we would end up in bed."

"Would that be so bad?" he asked smiling at her.

"Not if you ended up there every night for the rest of our lives." Rycca smiled back at him.

"That is entirely a possibility." Dan gently caressed her face and kissed her again.

The band played another set and they danced to each and

every song from their teenage years as they sang along. The food was put out and they ate and talked with fellow class-mates. The band played on and they danced into the early morning.

They walked to their cars at one in the morning.

"Would you care to stop by my house for a glass of wine or a cup of coffee?" Rycca asked as she got into her car.

"Thought you'd never ask." Dan followed her home.

Once inside her house, Rycca poured them each a glass of wine. They barely took one sip when he kissed her and they made their way up the staircase to her bedroom. Clothes came off piece by piece until they were both naked on her king size bed. Their bodies were on fire for each other. It had been way too long for both of them and they relished every passion-filled moment.

Rycca woke to a beautiful sunny summer day. She was in love for the second time in her life, with a guy who was oh so easy on the eyes and oh so nice. She watched him sleeping next to her.

"Hello beautiful," he said waking up. "You were the hottest woman at the reunion."

"I bet you say that to all your women."

"Can't say I do. You were definitely the hottest woman at the reunion."

"Really? You're just saying that," Rycca beamed at him and kissed him. "But thanks, anyway."

"I'm serious. No one came close to you. And I was the luckiest man there."

Rycca couldn't believe how lucky she was. Dan rolled over her and they made love again. Afterwards they lay together with Rycca's head on his chest as he gently caressed her back.

"Hey, we have a date today." He got up and put on his

clothes. "I'm going to go home to shower and change. I'll pick you up at eleven."

"I'll be ready."

Rycca showered and dressed. She was glowing. She wasn't sure if someone could fall in love this fast, but she was sure she was in love. He was perfect for her. Someone or something had gone to a lot of work to get them together. She was thankful to whoever it was. Running into each other on three different occasions in less than a week couldn't be coincidence.

Dan felt like the luckiest man alive. He had met a woman with whom he could spend the rest of his life. What were the odds he would run into her three times in one week purely by accident? Someone wanted them together and he wasn't about to say no. A part of him thought that maybe his late wife was up in heaven trying to find someone for him to love and share the rest of his life with. He wouldn't put it past her. She'd told him at the end she wanted him to be happy and find someone after she was gone. And he totally liked the woman she picked.

CHAPTER 5

At Lord Fletcher's, Rycca and Dan sat at a table overlooking Lake Minnetonka. They were famished and sampled almost everything on the buffet. They were both happy. For dessert they both opted for the summer special, S'mores Ice Cream Sandwiches. The graham crackers filled with toasted marshmallows and vanilla ice cream, were dipped in chocolate and then frozen. On a warm summer day they were delicious.

"Dan, I do have a question though. How many dates have you gone on from matches on the Metro Singles Dating site?"

Dan laughed. "None. How about you?"

"None. I didn't even actually sign up. My girlfriends, Shelly and Tara, thought I should start dating again, so they signed me up on the 4th of July. I have to say I was a bit surprised to see your face come up as my number one match."

"I was equally surprised to see your picture come up as my number one match." Dan smirked. "Some of my friends suggested it so I thought I would give it a shot since I was having a difficult time meeting quality women."

"Quality women?"

"Remember I told you I was in management at the bank?"

Rycca nodded. "You're not?"

"Rycca, I'm the president of the bank."

"Oh."

"Most women just want to go out with me because of my social status and income. I want someone who wants to go out with me because they like me."

"I like you. Now I *really* like you! Just kidding. Money is nice, but I need to like the person first. Guess I hit the jackpot."

Dan laughed. "Don't take this the wrong way, but I think my late wife was looking out for me from up above. Someone went to great lengths to get us together. It's almost as if they weren't taking any chances. I have a feeling I'm going to be thanking God every day for bringing us together."

"Sometimes things happen for reasons we don't understand. Even though I knew my ex had a roving eye, I was devastated when he left. I thought my life would never be the same. But if he hadn't left, I wouldn't have been able to meet you. And if it hadn't been such a difficult divorce, I wouldn't have insisted on getting the stupid boat just so he couldn't have it. After all the anxiety the stupid boat caused me, it was a means to an end. If I hadn't taken it out, we might not have met. But then again we would have met on the dating site. Oh, and then we would have met at the reunion. I think we were destined to be together."

"My sentiments exactly." Dan reached across the table to hold her hand as they silently watched the boats docking in Lord Fletcher's marina.

Rycca smiled at Dan. She'd found someone she could

definitely spend a lifetime with and she would be forever thankful she'd won the stupid boat in the divorce settlement. And the internet dating site? Maybe a little bit thankful. As for the twenty year class reunion, forever thankful because she'd had the time of her life!

S'mores Ice Cream Sandwiches

Ingredients

- 8 graham crackers, halved
- 8 regular size Hershey's chocolate bars
- 1 tablespoon butter
- 16 large marshmallows
- 2 cups vanilla ice cream

Instructions

1. Place graham crackers on a cookie sheet. Place a halved marshmallow on each half cracker. Broil in oven until marshmallows are lightly browned.
2. Melt chocolate bars with butter in microwave in a medium-sized bowl for about 1 minute. Heat for an additional minute if needed.
3. Scoop about ¼ cup vanilla ice cream on 8 of the cracker halves. Immediately cover with remaining halves to make 8 sandwiches. Dip sandwich into chocolate about half ways down on each sandwich. Place on a cookie sheet that has been covered with waxed paper.
4. Freeze for several hours before serving. Makes 8.

ABOUT THE AUTHOR

ROSE MARIE MEUWISSEN

Rose Marie Meuwissen, a first-generation Norwegian American born and raised in Minnesota, always tries to incorporate her Norwegian heritage into her writing. After receiving a BA in Marketing from Concordia University, a Masters in Creative Writing from Hamline University soon followed. Minnesota is still where she calls home.

She has traveled around the world, including Scandinavia, but still has many places to see, enjoys attending Scandinavian events, writing conferences and is usually busy writing Minnesota Lakes Contemporary Romances, Viking Time Travel Romances or Norwegian Traditions Children's Books.

NOVELS:

Taking Chances—a contemporary romance novel set in Minnesota and Arizona.

Married by Saturday—a contemporary romance novel set in Minnesota and Montana.

Looking for Mr. Right—a contemporary internet dating romance novel set on Prior Lake in Minnesota—***Coming soon!***

NOVELLAS:

Annika—A Christmas Romance—a contemporary romance set in Minnesota with a Nordic theme during the Christmas Holidays.

Skol! Viking Blonde Ale—a contemporary romance set in Minnesota at an Autumn festival complete with a fortune teller, ale and Vikings!

Choosing to Live—a Norwegian woman's journey during WWII to survive the Nazi Occupation of Norway—*Coming soon!*

ANTHOLOGIES:

A Date for Valentine's Day—a short romance set at Lafayette Country Club on Lake Minnetonka, Minnesota available in the anthology, ***Romancing the Lakes of Minnesota—Valentine's Day.***

Dance of Love—a short romance set at the Renaissance Fair in Shakopee, Minnesota, available in the anthology, ***Festivals of Love***.

Dancing in the Moonlight—a short romance set on Mille Lacs Lake, Minnesota available in the anthology, ***Love in the Land of Lakes***.

A Kiss Under the Northern Lights—a short romance set in Ely, Minnesota available in the anthology, ***Northern Kisses.***

CHILDREN'S BOOKS—REAL NORWEGIAN'S SERIES:

Real Norwegians Eat Lutefisk—a Children's book about the tradition of Lutefisk presented in both English and Norwegian.

Real Norwegians Eat Rømmegrøt—the second Children's book in the series about the tradition of Rømmegrøt presented in both English and Norwegian.

Real Norwegians Eat Lefse—the third Children's book in the series about the tradition of Lefse presented in both English and Norwegian.

Real Norwegians Eat Krumkake—the fourth Children's book in the series about the tradition of Krumkake presented in both English and Norwegian—*Coming next!*

NOVELETTES—COMING SOON!

Hot Summer Nights—a Summer romance set in Prior Lake, Minnesota on Prior Lake.

Railroad Ties—an Autumn romance set in Two Harbors, Minnesota on Lake Superior.

Blizzard of Love—a Winter romance set in Lutsen, Minnesota on Lake Superior.

Nor-Way to Love—a Spring romance set in Minneapolis, Minnesota on Lake Harriet.

Old Yule Log Fires—a Christmas romance set in Excelsior, Minnesota on Lake Minnetonka.

MICRO-MINI NOVELETTE—COMING SOON!

Christmas Notes—a collection of Christmas prose poems to warm the heart during the Christmas season.

PREVIEW

Continue Reading for a Preview of:

SKOL! VIKING BLONDE ALE

Fortunes, Love & Fate Series

Rose Marie Meuwissen

PREVIEW COPYRIGHT

SKOL! VIKING BLONDE ALE

Print Edition
Copyright 2020 by Rose Marie Meuwissen

Skol! Viking Blonde Ale is a work of fiction. Names, characters, and incidents depicted in this book are products of the author's imagination or are used fictitiously. Any resemblance to actual events, locales, organizations, or persons, living or dead, is entirely coincidental and beyond the intent of the author or the publisher. No part of this book may be reproduced or transmitted in any form or by any means, electronic or mechanical, including photocopying, recording, or by any information storage and retrieval system, without permission in writing from the publisher.

NO GHOSTWRITERS WERE USED IN THE CREATION OF THIS BOOK. This work of fiction is 100% the original work of Rose Marie Meuwissen.

ISBN 978-0-9903788-3-9

PREVIEW COPYRIGHT

Published in the United States of America
Nordic Publishing LLC
Cover Design by Raine English

SKOL! VIKING BLONDE ALE

FORTUNES, LOVE & FATE SERIES

Inga was living the dream, planning events for her own company, Unique Events, but she still hadn't found a guy who could be 'The One' for her. She never would've believed a fortune from a gypsy fortune teller promising her a 'love that surpasses time' could come true.

Erik moved from Norway to Minnesota to expand his Nordic Brewing company in the U. S. He'd promised himself to devote all his time to the business, but how was he to know that an unknown force of fate would introduce him to a woman he couldn't walk away from?

Their attraction could not be denied because ultimately, they were destined to be together. But could the Atlantic Ocean keep them apart? Would that even be possible if they were truly soul mates?

INGA'S FORTUNE:

FORTUNES, LOVE & FATE

Someone from your past will reappear in your life.
Your true soul mate.
With him, you will experience a love that surpasses time.

PROLOGUE

James J. Hill Days in Wayzata on Lake Minnetonka
September

Inga pulled into the back-parking lot of Main Street
Books at six. She couldn't believe it wasn't later. Friday
night rush hour traffic on the 494 Freeway was
bumper to bumper all the way from Eden Prairie to Wayzata.
The weather was still holding its summer like temps and true
Minnesotans would never pass up a beautiful autumn
weekend to go up North to their cabins one last time before
winter arrived. Today was the James J. Hill Days celebration
in Wayzata and the main street was packed with people as
she made her way into the book store to find her *Romancing
the Lakes of Minnesota* book club. This month instead of their
regular meeting, they planned to enjoy walking around and
checking out the celebration. Probably was a good call, she
thought, since it would've been difficult to hold their

meeting in the crowded book store and the activity outside would've been immensely distracting.

"Am I the last one to arrive?" Inga asked as she approached the book club group standing in front of the latest arrival shelf where the romance section was located.

"Bet the traffic was awful," Nora stated.

"Ready, to brave the crowds?" Katie asked.

"I'm hungry and thirsty, let's go!" Violet said.

Inga nodded in agreement and followed the group out the door to Main Street. They made their way down the street stopping at booths to look at the novelties for sale until finally, they stopped at the end of the street where the most unusual trailer was parked. The sign above the open door read, 'Fortune Teller'. It appeared to be Vintage, but these days they could make anything look old, even if it was new. Although, she had to admit, she'd never seen anything like it before, even though she'd been to many events. After all, she was an event planner. Intrigued was putting it mildly. Unfortunately, there was no stopping her curiosity. So, she entered the trailer.

"Come in, please," a very thickly accented voice beckoned from inside the trailer.

"Hello." Inga ducked and stepped into the trailer, taking in all the antiques and draped surroundings.

"Take a seat," the lady in gypsy like garb directed. "Let me see what your life has in store for you."

Inga didn't believe in fortune telling, at least she didn't think she did, but what could it possibly hurt to oblige the lady. It might be worth a laugh later, so she sat down on the partially pulled out chair at the table.

The fortune teller took the seat across from Inga and reached for her hand.

Slowly, Inga extended her hand. When their hands touched, Inga felt a strange sensation flow through her entire body, almost like a spark of electricity. It only lasted a few seconds and then was gone. She had no idea what it was or what caused it, but she finally relaxed.

The woman's face seemed deep in thought and completely fixated on her hand. "You are a very special lady. Very strong and independent. I see happiness in your future."

"Do you see a man?" Inga wasn't sure why'd she'd asked that particular question.

"Yes." The woman continued staring at her hand. "A very handsome man."

"Well, there certainly are enough good-looking men around. What I need is one that is interested in me long enough to stick around for a while."

"You have not met '*The One*' yet."

"When? When will it happen? I'm getting really tired of waiting around for him."

"Soon."

"So, is that my fortune?"

"No." The woman hesitated, then picked up a piece of paper and wrote a few lines down on it. She handed it to Inga. "This is your fortune: ***Someone from your past will reappear in your life. Your true soul mate. With him, you will experience a love that surpasses time.***"

"Great. But I'm sorry, I don't believe in magic."

"That's okay you don't have to believe. It will happen anyway."

Their eyes locked for a moment.

Inga got up to leave. "How much do I owe you?" Inga asked.

"For you, no charge. I've been waiting for you."

"I don't understand."

The fortune teller waived her hand in a shooing motion, indicating Inga was done and should leave.

As Inga stepped out of the trailer, Katie rushed up the steps. "My turn."

"So, what do you think? Is the Fortune Teller legit?" Violet asked.

"What kind of a question is that? Of course, it's not real. No one can tell another person what will happen in their future," Stephanie said.

"Care to share?" Nora asked.

Inga handed the piece of paper to Violet, who in turn handed it to Stephanie, who in turn handed it to Gwen and lastly to Nora.

"At least it's a good fortune. Let's hope it comes true," Stephanie said.

"Come on, you're not buying into this stuff, are you?" Inga shook her head.

Minutes later, Katie came down the trailer's steps, paper in hand grinning from ear to ear.

Violet practically ran to the steps to be next.

Each romance book club member shared their fortune while the next one took their turn. Being romantics at heart, they were all thrilled to find romance in their fortunes.

They continued strolling leisurely down the other side of the street where the craft brewery tents were located.

Inga spotted a tent with *Nordic Brewing* as the name. She selected it out of the five tents because of her love for all things Nordic and Viking. In fact, the Viking Ship logo caught her eye first. She walked up to the counter to see the menu more closely.

"What can I get you?"

Inga looked up quickly when she heard the strong Norwegian accented English and to her surprise saw almost a 'Thor' look alike, only his blonde hair was shorter. He could very well be from Viking blood, she thought. *Tall, muscular, with a chiseled face. Have I just died and gone to Valhalla?*

"What can I get you?" he repeated smiling broadly at her.

"What would you suggest?" she managed to get out. "I've never tried your brand before."

"For you lovely lady, I'd suggest the Viking Blonde Ale."

"Sounds absolutely perfect."

He turned his broad toned back toward her stretching the black T-shirt taut against his muscles and filled a plastic souvenir cup with Valhalla printed on one side and a picture of a Viking on the other side.

Inga pulled a five-dollar bill from her purse and set it on the counter. He handed her the cup instead of setting it down and her fingers lightly brushed his in the process. *There it was again.* A shiver of sorts shimmied its way through her body.

"Thank you, hope you enjoy it," he said as he picked up the money to put in the cash register.

"Thanks, I'm sure I will," Inga said while her eyes lingered on this modern-day Viking man. She felt sad that she would most likely not ever see him again. *Oh well, one can only wish.* She turned and walked away spotting her friends up ahead at a different craft brewery tent.

www.ingramcontent.com/pod-product-compliance
Lightning Source LLC
Chambersburg PA
CBHW022053170626
46808CB00003B/1453